# THE DAY THE SUN SPOKE

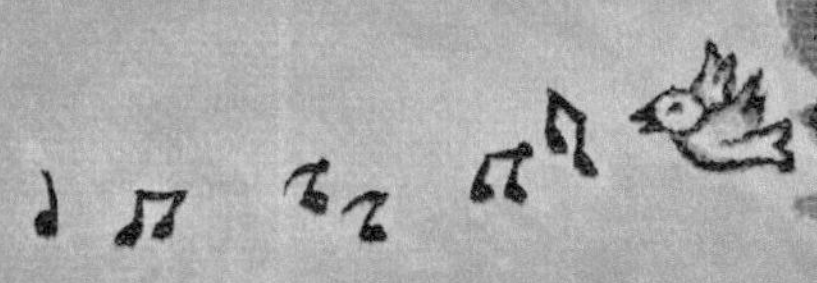

KATE WINNIE

ILLUSTRATED BY LIZETTE DUVENAGE

First Printing: 2014
ISBN 978-0-9903959-0-4

A book is never written by a single author for it takes a community to stitch together all the pieces of fabric that form the collective work. I extend my deepest gratitude to all that helped to make this book possible.

# Contents

Dear Reader,

When I was a child, I often heard stories in my mind as I slept. Sometimes, if I held tightly to the words, I could still continue the story as my eyes fluttered to awaken. The twelve stories you are about to read may just be a collection of tales I heard as a child. I'm not sure. But I do know they are stories that are meant to be shared! As Hans Christian Andersen is quoted as saying, "I have written them exactly the way I would tell them to a child."

These stories are an extension of my heart. I hold a firm belief that our planet is a place where Love in all things can truly exist. You as the reader have a part to play in this journey. As you listen to, or read aloud the stories, I encourage you to insert yourself directly into the storyline and contemplate how you would interact with the characters. Would you make the same choices or follow a different path? In each moment, we all have the ability to decide for ourselves the role we will play and the personality we will portray to others.

This discovery of your true self awaits you . . . . Let us begin!

In Love and Light,

Kate Winnie

# The Girl Who Flew with the Birds

Once upon a time there was a little girl who wanted to fly with the birds. But everyone told her that she couldn't, so not even once did she try. Then one day a villager came to the home of this little girl and he asked for the little girl's help. He needed someone to climb a tree for he had become frail and could no longer climb the ladder to pick the pears that he sold at the daily market. The young girl was strong and agile and could easily scale the tree without the help of the ladder. Despite the old man's insistence, she did not use the ladder.

As she climbed, the branches that she stepped on, oh some might say it was miraculous, some might say it was fate, but whatever the reason, the branches snapped and broke once her foot left and climbed to the next branch.

Higher and higher she went not realizing all things beneath her had disappeared. Even the old man had vanished. There she was at the top of the tree, basket full of pears, and no way to get down.

The little girl looked around and she saw things she had never seen before. Mountain tops, valleys, sights so beautiful tears filled her eyes. The world was majestic. The world was larger than she had ever known.

When night began to fall, the little girl looked down and it was then that she truly noticed there was no way down. The branches had fallen, lying in a pile at the bottom of the tree. The old man was gone and there was no one in sight. The little girl did not know what to do. For what does one do when you get to the top of a tree and the path that has led you to this spot has vanished?

Only somewhere buried deep within she knew what to do. For when you have a desire, it never truly disappears. You bury it, you hide it, you run from it, but it is always there with you waiting for the day when you take the leap, climb the highest mountain and step off. Only you don't fall . . . . you fly! That little girl took one last step off the branch and she flew.

She flew to all the places she had been looking at like those mountain tops, the rivers, and the lakes. She flew over the top of her house where her mother sat in the kitchen waiting for her daughter to come home.

She flew for as long as she could and when it was time to go home, she landed softly at the doorstep of her mother's home. She walked in with a basket full of pears and a smile as bright as the day that had just dawned.

No one ever believed her when she told the story of the day she climbed one of the tallest pear trees. How the tree had somehow dropped its branches and all that was left to do was to fly in order to get down. No one ever believed the story, but it did not matter. It did not matter for she had followed her heart. She had listened to the drum that had always beat within her. The one that told her she could fly . . . and she did.

# The Boy Who Could See All

Once upon a time there was a boy who could not understand why he could not see. He had been born blind. His mother and his father took him to the home of a wise man and asked, "Why can our son not see?" Everyone in the village knew this man was the wisest among them and so the parents asked him for his guidance. The man asked for the young boy to be brought forward and he placed his wrinkled, but strong hand on the boy's forehead. He asked the boy, "Son, what do you see? What do YOU see?" The boy had never been asked this question before. He had always been told that he was blind, that he could see nothing. But that was not the truth. The truth was he could see everything. He could see the wind. He could see the bird's song. He could see the rain beating against the window.

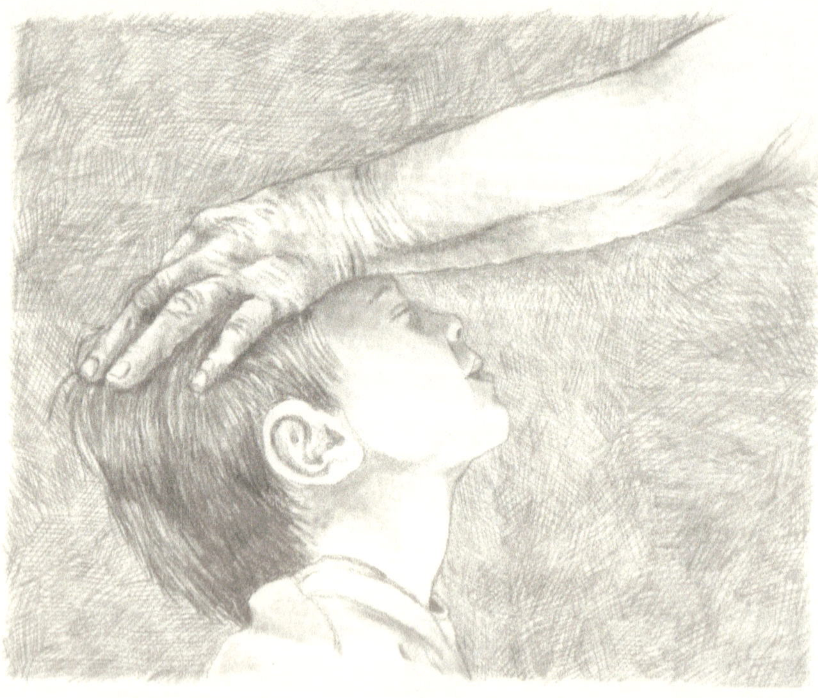

He could see all things, because in all things, you can see. Not with your eyes, but with your heart. Deep inside your heart is this knowing. This young boy could see all.

The wise man turned to the young boy's mother and father and he spoke in a harsh voice. "Open your eyes! For your son sees what you have not seen. Listen with your heart and know that all things are here for you to see and know."

The young boy walked home holding the hands of his mother and father. He saw the trees swaying in the breeze. He saw the sun shining from above and he saw the birds fluttering here and there and saying hello. He never again asked why he could not see for now he knew that he could see how so many have forgotten. Now it is time for us all to see; to see with the guidance from our hearts.

# The Girl Who Was Afraid of Everything

Once upon a time there was a little girl who was afraid of everything. When she walked, she was afraid she would fall. When she ran, she was afraid she would never stop. When she climbed, she was afraid the mountain would not hold her. When she heard the wind whisper her name, she was afraid it was not real. This little girl was afraid of everything. Everything frightened her.

One day, the sun began to descend which happens every day at a certain hour, but not this day. The sun started to descend at an hour when everyone was busy going about their daily lives. Everyone was going here and there relying on the sun to provide the light they needed to do their work. Only on this day, as they were busy going here and there, the sun's light began to slowly fade as if it was nightfall. People in the village began to point and cry out, "Why is the sun leaving us? Where is the light going? Will we be in darkness?" Before long, the light was gone. The sun had set and everywhere there was blackness.

The little girl who was afraid of everything was walking from her home to a nearby village to fetch something for her mother. As she walked, she became aware of the fading light. Only instead of being afraid, she was curious for she knew that the sun always rose and set at a certain time and in a certain way and that this day was different. As the wind whispered her name, she spoke out and asked, "Why is the sun fading? Where is the light going? How will I find my way to where I am headed?"

On that day with chaos everywhere, people running here and there and crying out in fear, that little girl found her way to where she was going. She found it in the darkness.

She found it by following something deep within her that told her to stay on the path. She knew which steps to take. She knew where there were cracks. She knew where she might slip and she made sure to stay on the path where she would be safe.

When you follow your path and you ignore any sign that might take you from it, you are always guided to where you need to go. This little girl reached the nearby village and the home of her mother's friend who was tucked away in her house frightened that the day had come when the sun would not shine again. But this little girl knew the light would return. The light would return and she too would return safely to her home for she knew the way now and she was not afraid.

Sometimes we live in darkness for a short time and we do not always know the reasons. Sometimes it is the work of our own doing. Sometimes it is something we cannot even begin to understand. But this little girl learned that day that when you listen, when you hear the wisdom of the wind, the stories told in the birds' songs, when you accept in your heart what you know to be true, you will always find your way. And light will always return.

# *The Woman Who Walked in the Morning Dew*

Once upon a time there was a woman who could hear the voice of Mother Earth. She heard the rumblings of the mountains in the distance and she knew what they spoke. She knew when the rooster crowed in the morning that the sun was rising and that the day would be glorious for the rooster told her what the day would bring. She would walk in the morning dew.

She walked in the morning dew and knew why she was here. Mother Earth spoke to her in whispers and songs and in moments she could not always understand. But she always knew there was someone with her; someone who stood beside her in her efforts to bring light to this world. She may not have known who it was, but it was Mother Earth who walked beside her in the morning dew. And it was Mother Earth who awakened the rooster, who awakened the sun, who began the day anew. It was Mother Earth who spoke from the mountain top; who sent the clouds; who sent the rain. It was Mother Earth who gave her the strength to walk in the morning dew.

# Jeremiah and the Tiger

There is a story that has been passed down from generation to generation that speaks of a time that comes in everyone's life when an animal will greet you at the threshold of the spirit world and accompany you as you return to the whole. There was a little boy named Jeremiah who heard this story from his grandfather, who had heard this story from his grandfather, who had heard this story from his grandfather, and so it went. Jeremiah wondered about the animal. He wondered which animal would greet him. Was it different for each person? Was it always the same?

This thought plagued his mind . . . in sleep, in play, in rest. He was always thinking about the animal. What animal would it be that would greet him when it was his time to meet the Creator?

Sometimes he would imagine that it was a grand lion, fierce and strong, and Jeremiah would ride its back holding firmly to the lion's mane. Sometimes he thought that perhaps it would be a butterfly and he too would soar high into the sky.

He never knew for sure which animal it would be, but then one day he had a dream while resting in a field outside the village. It was a very vivid dream. A dream that when you awake, you think it has really happened.

Jeremiah dreamt of being in an open space surrounded by trees. He dreamt that it was peaceful there and then in the distance, in an opening in the trees, emerged a tiger. The tiger came forward and laid its head upon Jeremiah's lap so peacefully that it was as if the tiger had fallen asleep. Jeremiah raised his hands and placed them upon the tiger's head. He glided his hands through soft fur and soaked in its exuberance for this tiger carried the spirit of ten thousand men. Just as Jeremiah too began to slip into a restful sleep, the tiger raised its head to meet the eyes of Jeremiah and spoke.

"Young Jeremiah, for years you have pondered the question, what animal will meet me at the end of my journey in this lifetime? Although it may be a question you greatly want answered, it has kept you from living a full life. Why should you want to answer a question about your fate when there is life to live? You, dear boy, are destined for such greatness. It is time to put aside these questions of what will happen then and begin living your life now. For in each moment there are lessons to learn and there are moments like this one to treasure and remember. When you laid your hand upon my head, you were showing all things how gentle life can be. Do not worry yourself with things that do not need to be understood. When the time is right you will know which animal will greet you at the threshold for that is where you will be. Today in this moment, you are a young man who is free to explore this grand world and live life to its fullest. Rise now and claim what is yours. This place will be here when you are ready for it. You will find it when it is time. Go forward Jeremiah. Go forward."

Jeremiah walked home that day and found his grandfather was no longer of this earth. His grandfather had lived a full and magnificent life. He was known among the villagers as a man who was connected to all things. Jeremiah knew that he too could be known in such a way. He wanted to be for he had now learned that if you take hold of the present moment, all things are available to you. That day, Jeremiah took hold. He took hold of his life. Now when he dreams he does not ponder questions of what will happen . . . he questions, "What can I do? What can I do now?"

# The Magic Pot

Once upon a time there was a young man who longed to live in the trees. As a young boy he often spent hours sitting atop the tallest tree and looking out at all there was to see. He would watch as the clouds shifted and moved in their way. He would watch as the birds soared from tree to tree, building their nests, feeding their young, and being a part of the whole. He would watch as the wind rose up and rustled the leaves causing the branches to sway back and forth, back and forth. It was in those moments that he felt such joy.

But it was always at the end of the day that his mother would call for him and he would leave the trees and return home. He would lay his head on his pillow and dream of when the day would come that he could live among the trees.

Years later a stranger came to the village. He was selling a magic pot. This pot was said to listen to all that you desire and place those desires into the palm of your hand. The young man heard from the villagers that the stranger was offering a good price, but they were too skeptical. They feared that if they should spend their money on something that might not work, the other villagers would laugh at them. They would be ashamed of doing something so foolish.

Those that the young man spoke with turned away as the stranger walked by. But the young man had been working hard and he had been saving. Saving for something he did not know, but he had been secretly putting aside a few coins so that when the moment was right he would have what he needed.

As the stranger walked by him, he called out, "Please stop, I wish to hear your tale." The stranger was just beginning to leave for he had heard that the villagers were not interested; that they were too afraid to buy something that was not for certain He saw that the young man seemed determined to speak to him and so he turned back down the path.

The stranger told his story of how the magic pot had served him well, but he felt it was time to offer this pot to someone else who may be in need. He had been traveling for some time now, sharing his story, and looking for someone who would hear him.

The young man told him that if he could just wait a short while he would run home for beneath his pillow was a bag of gold that would be enough to pay for the pot.

When the young man returned he gave the stranger all that he had. It might have been even more than was needed, but he gave all that he had. He gave all that he had so that when he spoke to the magic pot and told of what he desired, he knew with all his heart that it would come true.

Years later an old man walked down this same path calling out to the villagers that he had a magic pot to sell. His story told of great adventures whilst living among the trees. A life full of such joy most could not understand of what he told. It spoke of desires most people dare not dream. The man said it was true, but most would not believe him. It was their fear that prevented them, that stopped them from hearing his truth. Among the villagers, there was one, maybe two who would listen to the story. Who would listen to the story and hear what they needed to hear. What we desire can always be found when we listen with our hearts and we follow the path that so few believe to be true.

# The Animals

The story goes that long ago it was only animals that walked this earth. When the time came for man to live among the animals, most chose to live on the outskirts. Animals were said to know all and man was just beginning to understand. There was said to be one who lived among the animals and understood them. You might think it was a man with the strength of ten; a man who walked with courage and ferocity. No, that was not the case. It was a young boy. A young boy lived among the animals and he was known as Running Bear.

The young boy could be seen racing alongside the cheetahs. The young boy could be seen dangling from the tree branches picking the oranges alongside the orangutans. The young boy could be seen wading through the stream with the hippopotamuses. Those who saw him believed he was not human. Many said he was some type of new animal because that would explain how he could run so fast, climb so high, and swim so deep. No, he was a human. He was a young boy who understood the wisdom of the animals. He understood that it was the animals who knew how to survive by using what Mother Earth had given them.

One day one of the villagers was walking along a path when a spider dropped down before him. The spider asked for a word with the man. This foolish man did not have ears that could hear and so he did not hear what the spider spoke. He only saw the spider before him, and being one who did not like what he could not understand, he squished it with his foot.

The next day a woman walked by carrying a basket of fruit on her head and another spider dropped down and asked if he might speak with her. This woman, unaware of even where she was stepping, did not see the spider and so she squished him too.

Later that afternoon, a child came along and a spider swooped down before the child and asked if he might speak with her. This child was young and her ideas were not as muddied as those who had come before her.

The child dropped down to her knees, put her ear to the ground, and she listened. She heard what no one else could hear. She heard that the water in the nearby river was going to rise and that if the townspeople did not move to higher ground they would be washed away in the flood. The little girl was warned of what would come and she was told what to do to be safe.

The girl thanked the spider and she walked home to find her mother preparing the day's meal. She started to share what she had been told but her mother would not listen. As soon as the little girl began the story, her mother held up her hands and shook her head. She said no spider could see the future – such silliness. The little girl tried to tell the story to her father, but he would listen no further than her mother for he too said a tiny creature could not know something he did not know.

The little girl left her home and walked to the edge of the village where there was a well. Many children had started to throw coins into the well believing that their wishes would come true. She took one of the coins her father had given her and closed her eyes. As she spoke aloud of what she had heard, she dropped the coin into the well hoping that those who needed to know would hear her and do what needed to be done.

Near that well was a tree and beneath that tree was a man who had awoken when he heard the voice of the little girl. He heard her story foretelling of danger and felt he needed to caution the village of what was to come. He walked from home to home sharing the girl's story.

Soon people were running here and there, shouting out to each other, gathering everything they could and carrying it all toward higher ground. When the man told the last person in the village, he turned and walked to the nearest hilltop and found a tree where he could fall back asleep.

The animals were grazing on this hilltop and watched as the village people moved all about. Even Running Bear stopped to observe the chaos. They watched as the townspeople gathered everything they could carry and more.

The villagers filled their bundles so full of belongings that they struggled to ascend the hillside. Some realized that they could not go on carrying these heavy bundles and so left them by the path and marched forward to safety.

Others could not part with what they had brought and so when the flood waters came they were washed away with their belongings. Some made it to safety and some did not.

When we choose to free ourselves from all things we do not need, our load is much lighter and our step is much quicker. Like the animals, it is easier to move where we are headed when we carry no more than we need.

The little girl who had been standing at the well watching turned and saw Running Bear with the animals grazing on the hilltop. She climbed the hilltop and joined him where the tall grass stood. The spider that had spoken to her earlier that day dropped down on her shoulder and spoke of how wise she was to follow her heart; to trust in what she heard and to know without a doubt that she would be safe.

# The Rising Sun

The rising sun is said to be revered by the native people of long ago. In one village, the people were said to rise just before dawn each morning and stand before the glorious sun and give thanks for all that they had. They gave thanks to the antelope for sacrificing their lives so they could eat. They gave thanks to the birds for sharing their songs and they gave thanks to the sun for providing them light.

There was one among them who was said to wake long before the sun rose in the sky. He would begin his day fumbling in the darkness to find his way. Sometimes he would light a candle instead of waiting for the sun to brighten the day. Now the reason he would wake before the others was so that he could be the first at the fishing hole to check the nets. He also knew where the best traps were set and he easily took more than his share.

When night would fall, the people would gather together to eat and give thanks for their day. While everyone gathered, this man would sneak off and find a dark spot to sleep. Sometimes the others talked about what to do for they were aware of what this man was doing. They meant him no harm but they worried what would happen to the man for he did not seem to worry about wandering around in the dark.

One day while the man was stumbling through the darkness on his way into the woods, he heard a distant rumbling. No one else was awake at this hour and so he was the only one who heard the noise. He could feel the tremors beneath his feet and he could feel within a deep sense of dread of what might come for it is not easy to see in darkness. As he stood there alone, seeing nothing, yet not knowing he was surrounded by everything, the man dropped to his knees and felt with his hands the turbulence from Mother Earth. Just as he dropped to his knees, he cried out asking to be saved.

Within a short time, he felt something warm heating the middle of his back. He turned and watched, for the first time in his life, as the sun began to rise.

He watched as the sun made its first appearance of the day and everything around him changed from dark to light. As the sun rose higher in the sky, the quieter the rumblings became. There this man was on his knees. The only thing still shaking was himself for he had been so frightened he would be lost in the darkness.

Now that the sun had risen, he could see that there was nothing to fear. He was safe, not far from his village, and everyone else was there surrounding him giving thanks for the new day. He too, rose to meet the sun and thanked with all his heart that the light had been returned and that he could begin this day anew.

# *The Land of Giants*

Once upon a time in a faraway place there lived a tribe of Giants. They were said to be so tall they could walk through clouds. There were many in the villages surrounding this land who lived in fear of the Giants. But the Giants were actually quite friendly. They were kind to all they met. They were careful to look where they stepped to avoid stomping on a flower or a bee buzzing by. In fact, the Giants lived in harmony; getting along with each other and all that was around them. Still, those who did not know them, feared them. In one village, there was a band of fiercely brave men who boasted that one day they would meet the Giants and conquer them.

One day, a story passed through that a nearby village had been destroyed. The rumor told of how the Giants had barreled through the village wrecking everything in sight. This rumor spread throughout the land, and before you knew it, many young men were said to be preparing for battle against the Giants. Soon stories were being told of how vicious the Giants were; saying they stole children from their mothers and burned down huts. These stories reached far and wide and before long a large army of men had formed to attack the Giants.

The Giants being so high to the sky had not heard the stories; nor would they have believed people would say such ill things of them. On the day the men came to their land, the Giants were taken quite by surprise for it was not common for village men to enter their land. Life had always been separate. Giants living high in the sky and men low to the earth.

That day the men rode into the Giants' land on horses and began shooting arrows into the air. The Giants were by far outnumbered and the men were relentless. So many had heard the stories and had come to seek revenge. But the truth is that the village that had been left in ruins had been hit by a sudden hailstorm. It could not have been stopped or prevented, but neither the Giants nor the men knew this.

As the Giants looked down on the men encircling them, you might think that they struck back. You might think they raised their gigantic arms and pounded the ground, crushing everything in sight . . . but they did not. No, the Giants lowered their heads to the ground to see and hear what was happening and were careful not to step on anyone. They spoke in but a whisper, but could be easily heard by the men, and asked why the men had come with such scornful looks armed with bows and arrows in their hands. What was it that the Giants had done?

All of the men started to talk at once, yelling and screaming, calling out "You know what you have done!" But the Giants were patient and they sought out one man who seemed to be holding back, not sure of why he was there but afraid to leave. One of the Giants offered him his hand so the man could climb up to speak face to face. The young man explained why so much hatred had been brought to their land. He explained what had happened and why the men believed it was the Giants' fault.

The Giants listened carefully and when the man's story was finished, the Giants turned and walked toward the village that had been left in ruins.

They stood before the destroyed land and asked the people to have faith that all could be restored. The Giants planted flowers beside the huts that were still standing and called to the storm clouds to offer the rain that would help the flowers to bloom even more angelic than before.

The men who had arrived so quickly at the doorstep of the Giants' land returned home with new stories. Some still insisted the Giants were dangerous and should be feared; while others told of how the Giants had helped to return beauty to the land. One man, among them, told of how he had touched the wisps of a cloud and that he knew with all his heart that there still remained good on this earth.

# Medicine Woman

This story begins in a place where it was common for young children to be raised to learn the ways of their grandparents. They learned beside their elders how to farm and hunt and make dinner over a fire. Some children were born with a gift for healing and were taught by a medicine person who knew how to grow and use the plants to heal. These children were chosen to work beside the medicine people and learn their wisdom and secrets.

In one village, there was a granddaughter born to a medicine woman. It was believed that this little girl would learn beside her grandmother the healing wisdom from the plants.

When she was born, her grandmother placed her hands upon her forehead and with a kiss she called on her powers to make it so. This little girl was born with a fiery energy and was always finding ways to escape her grandmother's lessons. She longed to see the world and so when she was fourteen years old, she packed all of her belongings in a bundle and set out to see the world. She wrote a note to her family and off she went.

She sailed across the ocean. She traveled to faraway lands. She saw things most cannot say they have ever seen. Anytime anyone would stop and ask her where she was headed she would always say she was headed toward her destiny. One day she was walking along a dirt path when she came across a garden. The smell of the roses called to her and so she set down her bundle and tilted her head to take in the fragrance of the roses. As she stood there admiring their beauty, a woman walked out and called to her asking where she was headed. Just as the young girl began to say what she always said, a strong wind blew across the garden sealing her lips shut. Again the older woman called out to ask where she was headed and just as she was about to speak the wind began to swirl and twirl and before she knew it her words where lost in the wind.

The old woman stepped down from her porch and walked to the young woman holding out her hand to ask if everything was okay. It was then that the wind started to blow so strongly that the young woman was lifted from the ground, twirling into the air, and carried off.

When she was set gingery back on the ground, she looked up to see a garden that looked almost familiar. Except there were no roses, or any other flowers to be seen. Everything was brown from being neglected over time. Yet, this garden seemed familiar; perhaps one she had played in when she was younger. When she looked up, there stood a woman who looked much like her grandmother. This woman had sad eyes and slumped shoulders as if she had worked too hard in her life.

The woman walked over to her and laid her hands on her shoulders and asked where she was headed. It was then that the young woman realized it was her mother that spoke to her and that it was her garden that had been neglected for so long.

You see her grandmother had passed away not long after she had left. Her mother had been carrying the burden of healing the villagers without anyone to help her for the wisdom had not been passed on to anyone else. It had always been the dream of the grandmother that her granddaughter would walk in her footsteps.

The young woman had always wanted to be separate from her place in the village. She wanted to go out into the world and see everything there was to see. Now that she had returned, she realized although she had an exciting and adventurous journey, her place was here and it was time to return to the whole. She was a part of this little village and this little village was a part of her.

# The Boy Who Was Loved
## By the Forest

Once upon a time there was a little boy who was so loved by the forest. But it was his curiosity in all things that made him misunderstood by those around him. It was difficult for many to understand why the little boy with the face of an angel would crawl on his knees and hide when others came to visit. His mother would hang her head in shame when people would stop and stare at the little boy. This little boy was so strong in spirit but he walked so alone here on this earth. His mother wondered what would become of him. She wondered if anyone would accept him in this world when he seemed so distant and detached from all that was expected of a young boy.

But what his mother did not know was that her son would someday grow up to be a great warrior. He would fight for all the wrong that was in the world. He would grow up to have a great impact in this world for his curiosity in all things was not something to fear.

When he crawled on his hands and knees he was not hiding, he was just looking at all things and seeing all things for what they were. He was searching for what lived deep within the ground that cannot be seen by human eyes but with the heart.

When he escaped into the woods, his mother thought he was alone, but it was the life within the forest that kept him company and shared its love for him.

It was in the time he spent in the forest that he learned the truth. He would one day stand above the landscape and call out to the wind to begin the change that was so desperately needed here on earth.

You see sometimes when we look at people and we see what is only on the outside, we do not see their true self. For the outside is only a glimpse of something much deeper that we all have within us. Like this young boy, we are all warriors meant to serve a great purpose on this earth. Some of us forever stay hidden while others among us walk with the wisdom of many lifetimes. There is nothing to be feared. This little boy always remembered what the forest had taught him; that there is love and light all around us and it is available to those of us who are conscious enough to look.

# *The Day the Sun Spoke*

This is a story of triumph. It is a story of defeat. It is a story that has yet to be told. Once upon a time in a village there lived a little girl who would pray every morning as the sun rose and every night as the sun set that all things would be beautiful. She did not wish for these things in a greedy way. She did not wish for her rags to turn to silk. Nor did she wish for her tattered hut to be turned to a golden palace. No, she wished for all things to be beautiful in the way that one sees beauty in the rain and the thunder, and the freshly fallen snow, and the leaves as they change from crimson to gold.

One night as the little girl knelt beside her bed and prayed she felt that her prayers had been answered. She felt that something or someone had heard her that had not listened before. A door had opened that had always been closed. She did not know why she felt this way but she was certain the world would look differently someday.

It was on that night, so long ago, while the moon was high in the sky that the sun asked for just one day, could all things return to what they were. For just one day, could the little girl see how it had been? For just one day, could *we* all see how it had been?

As you know, there was a time when the buffalo roamed free; when the world was new and there was beauty all around us. The birds would share their songs with us and we would be as One.

But in time things started to change. Things that were once beautiful were taken down, pushed aside, to make room for what man thought would make life easier. New buildings were constructed. Trains and planes take us from one land to another. New technology is developed every day to make it easier for us to stay connected; and yet, we no longer remember we are a part of the bird's song or the trees as they grow and mature. We no longer remember we are a part of the lakes as they flow from one body of water to another.

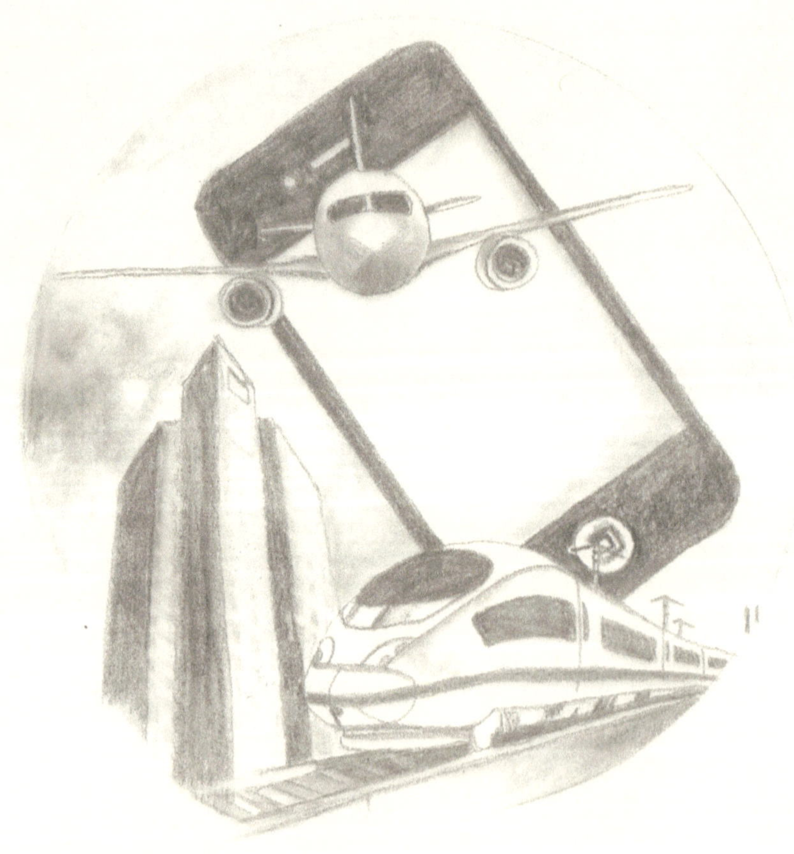

We believe we are separate from many things and so if that little girl was here today, and perhaps she is in some way, she would still be asking if all things could be beautiful again.

Today as you read this story, it is time for all things to be connected in the way they once were. In the way that the birds would sing and we would know their song. In the way that we once shared with the trees and spoke of our day. It was then that we were truly connected for all things knew what was said by another. You, the reader, can do your part to show everyone how together we can live as One. You can call good morning to the sparrow as he flies overhead. You can plant in a garden the vegetables that will know you by name.

You can learn to treat all things with respect, no matter how large or how small. In doing these things, you the reader, can share your light and the beauty we have forgotten will shine brightly once more.